A CHRISTMAS WISH FOR CORDUROY

A CHRISTMAS WISH FOR CORDUROY

Story by B. G. Hennessy
Pictures by Jody Wheeler
Based on the characters created by Don Freeman

SCHOLASTIC INC.

For my sister and brother, who know all about how Christmas feels —BGH

For Betty and Byrhl, who made each Christmas feel like magic for us —JHW

To Lydia and Nora, for lending a helping hand —The Freeman Foundation

ISBN 978-0-545-93533-3

12 11 10 9 8 7   18 19 20/0

Printed in the U.S.A.   40

First Scholastic printing, December 2015

All of the author's royalties from the sale of *A Christmas Wish for Corduroy* goes to the Lydia Freeman Charitable Foundation to support psychological care and research concerning children with disabilities, severe illnesses, or trauma.

For more information, please visit the Lydia Freeman Charitable Foundation website at: http://www.lfcf.info/home.html

Purchase of this book is not tax deductible.

Set in LTC Cloister
The art for this book was created using scratchboard and colored inks.

One December afternoon, a toy bear in a big store was just waking up when he heard a mother asking a boy, "Have you decided what you would like for Christmas yet?"
The bear sat a little taller and perked up his ears. Maybe this boy wanted a bear!

But the boy zipped right by him and pointed to a bright red, shiny fire engine. "I'm going to ask Santa for a fire truck with a big ladder and a bell!" the boy said.

The bear watched sadly as the boy walked away.

In the store that afternoon, the book at story time was about Santa and the elves at the North Pole. All the children were excited to make Christmas lists and visit Santa.

"Maybe I should visit Santa," the bear thought. "I could ask him if he knows a girl or boy who wants a bear. Tonight I'll go see if I can find him."

Just before closing time, a girl stopped right in front of the bear.

"Maybe she wants a bear!" he hoped.

But the girl pointed to a doll in a pink dress. "Mommy, look!
A Pretty Piper doll! That is the doll I am going to ask Santa
to bring me when I see him."

"Make sure you put her name on your list, dear," said her mother.

"And if you are going to see Santa, we should get you a special outfit."

"A special outfit? I didn't know I needed a special outfit to see Santa," thought the bear as he looked at his brown fur. "Why, I don't have any clothes at all! And without a name, how can I ever be on anyone's Christmas list?"

Late that evening, when all the shoppers had gone home, the bear climbed down from his shelf.

The store seemed much bigger without any people in it. There were strange shadows everywhere. The bear felt very small.

He found a department that sold hats. "Those hats look pretty special," he said.

He tried on all kinds of hats, but none of them seemed quite right for a bear who was looking for Santa.

Next to the hat department was the shoe department. "A pair of shiny new shoes would make me look special," thought the bear. But all the shoes were much too big.

Then he spotted the children's clothes department. Surely he would find an outfit there. But the only clothes his size were the baby clothes! So the bear kept looking.

Up ahead he saw a sign with Santa's picture on it.

"This must be the way to the North Pole!" he said. "That's just where

I want to go."

He followed the signs until he almost bumped into a reindeer.

"The North Pole looks exactly like it did in the book," said the bear. There were trees with reindeer and a workshop for Santa. He went inside to take a look.

"This is a very little workshop," said the bear. He sat down in a chair. It was the perfect size. He looked around the room. There were small toys, tools, and even some elf clothes hanging on the wall. That gave him an idea.

First he tried on an elf hat, but his ears were too small.
Then he tried on a pair of elf shoes, but his furry bear paws
were too big.

Finally he tried on the elf clothes. They fit perfectly.
Now unbuttoning and buttoning anything with bear paws is not
easy, and one button almost fell off before the bear finally got
the overalls on.

"These overalls are just the right kind of special for me," thought the bear as he looked at himself in a mirror. "Now I am ready to meet Santa."

Then he noticed a big chair nearby. "That must be Santa's chair!" said the bear. "I will wait here so I will be first in line when Santa comes, and then I can ask him for a little girl or boy to take me home."

By now it was very late, and the bear was very tired. He climbed up onto the chair, and before too long he was fast asleep.

That is exactly where Santa found him the next morning.
"Good morning, little fellow! How did you get up on my chair?"
asked Santa. "Those are some mighty fine green corduroy overalls
you are wearing. A good-looking bear like you should be with the
other toys.

"Mrs. Claus, would you please bring Corduroy back to the toy
department?" asked Santa.

"Santa called me Corduroy," thought the bear. "I have a name!
Now I can be on someone's Christmas list."
The bear was finally ready to tell Santa his Christmas wish.

But before Corduroy could say a word, he was on his way back to the toy department with Mrs. Claus. Past the clothes, past the shoes, and past the hats, farther and farther away from Santa, until he was back where he started.

"We found Corduroy bear on Santa's chair this morning," Mrs. Claus explained to the saleslady. "Doesn't he belong in your department?"

The saleslady looked at Corduroy in his new green overalls. "You do look familiar," she said as she put him back on the shelf.

That is just where Corduroy bear was later that day when a mother and daughter walked into the toy department.

The little girl stopped and looked straight into Corduroy's bright eyes. "Oh, Mommy!" she said. "Look! There's the very bear I've always wanted!"

Her smile made Corduroy feel more special than all the names and outfits combined.

"This must be what Christmas feels like," thought Corduroy, and he smiled his best bear smile right back.